LOST & FOUND

Lost & Found

David Lanier

Texas Review Press
Huntsville, Texas

FIRST EDITION, 2013
Requests for permission to reproduce material from this work should be sent to:

Permissions
Texas Review Press
English Department
Sam Houston State University
Huntsville, TX 77341-2146

Acknowledgements:

Grateful acknowledgement is made to the following publications, where several of these poems first appeared, some in a slightly different version:

Antietam Review	Skin-The-Cat
GSU Review	Mrs. Luna
Louisville Review	The Splinter
	While We Wait For The Demerol To Work
	White Hibiscus
Marlboro Review	Infidelities
Poet Lore	My Mother, Trimming Hedges
River Oak Review	Lost Bird
	The Upright
Southern Poetry Review	Ramon
The Sow's Ear	Bright Leaf
Tar River Poetry	One Morning

"What A Penny Bought" was published in *Hungry As We Are: An Anthology of Washington Poets*, ed. Ann Darr.

"Night Watch" was published in *Articulations: The Body and Illness in Poetry*, ed. Jon Mukand.

Cover image, *Lost & Found*, by Stephen Wagner (used with permission)

Library of Congress Cataloging-in-Publication Data

Lanier, David, 1948-
  [Poems. Selections]
  Lost & found / David Lanier.
    pages cm.
  Poems.
  ISBN 978-1-937875-04-6 (paperback : alk. paper)
  I. Title. II. Title: Lost and found.
  PS3612.A58538L67 2013
  811'.6--dc23
                    2013013293

to the memory of my mother,
Evelyn Eadon Lanier
(1919 - 2007)

Contents

LOST & FOUND

MY MOTHER, TRIMMING HEDGES

Finding you this evening
where I've never found you,
at the far end of the yard,

halfway up a ladder, doing work
my father always did,
I become suddenly shy

and younger than I am. From here,
the long stretch of your body
hovers above the ordinary

hedge. Arms, strong, flexed,
beat a steady rhythm at your sides.
I'd like to remember you

like this, lifting out
of the dense water oaks along
South Howard Circle

that become in the thinning light
almost transparent,
a Chagall musician rising above

Methodist spires and rows
of houses square as gunshell
boxes, until you soar

out of the reach of family
and neighbors who come to dark
windows and whispers. I'd like

to be here when you look back
from afar and see
for once your house, your life

no longer a nest of clinging
shadows
but a garden lit by spirit lamps

whose light spreads out
like the first clear
dew that settles on our hedges.

ONE MORNING

What he saw first, eye-level
in the shiny belly of the coffeepot
was his own face grown enormous,
how it had pushed aside the doors
of cabinet and refrigerator, how
the floor receded away from him
across misshapen squares of kitchen tile
to a window so small it permitted only
a single shaft of sunlight to enter.
To his left, a set of miniature chairs
brooded around the mushroom-size table.
And to the right was his mother—thin curve
of pink and yellow housecoat, miles away
at the end of the counter—her voice
(telling him *again* to take his seat)
so faint he barely heard it above
the pop and sizzle of the stove, the rheumy
coughing of the coffeepot. All around
him aromas were assembling.
But for the moment he was stalled
at the periphery of appetite, content
just to stare into the round pools
of his own eyes, in that spot where
the world seemed to circle around his head
as long as he held perfectly still.

HAY FEVER

It would wait for a moonless September night,
when everyone was sleeping, to escape
from my grandfather's barn and make its way

to town. I'd be wakened in the morning
by the sound of the bus hissing to a stop
at the foot of our hill, just to let Hay Fever off.

Then I could hear it crossing the field next
to our house, whispering to itself about itself.
Impolite, almost rude I thought, the way

it showed up each year uninvited, managed
somehow to slip past Mother who stood guard
by the front door, armed with dust cloth

and disinfectant. I knew it had me when
my bedroom walls exploded into loud snorts
and sneezes, when I sniffed the odor

of wet wool and feathers. It locked an arm
around my chest and long raw fingers
began to claw the back of my throat, to rub

one eye until I wept. Throughout the day,
even at school, it refused to let go, kept
tickling my nose, plugging up my ears.

In the evening, after Mother's pill, I
watched it spread a ceilingful of stars
over my bed. And just before I fell asleep,

listened to it prowling the neighborhood,
fumbling at locks: low, insistent
thump of gypsy moths against the narrow

screen, growl of wind through weeds
outside my window—the place it
gathered strength, waited out the night.

THE SPLINTER

Seated at the opposite end of the sofa,
circled in lamplight, she won't
look at his face as she cleans
her needle up and down
with alcohol on cotton ball,

strikes a match, plunges the needle's point
into the blue-bright flame. It's as if
she can't hear him, or will only
answer the cries by gripping
his ankle a little tighter
each time he tries to yank away.
The look on her face betrays
no fear or anger, only a weariness
as she rubs the antiseptic swab
in wider and wider rings
spreading out from the dark
business planted deep under sweet skin.

Suddenly she says *hold still*, moves
the needle. Then just as quickly
halts, her needle fixed mid-air,
silence applied between them
like a tourniquet pinching off
his need to resist, her will
to dig in. And is it his foot or her
upraised hand that first begins
to tremble, as each tries to unimagine
the small rose of blood that will bloom
at the point needle enters flesh?

WORDS

for my brother

We thought Mother had a name
for anything capable of causing us
trouble: chicken pox, head lice,
growing pains, the flu. With one
hand on our forehead or tummy,
she could say what was wrong with us
even before we knew we were sick.

She had no word, though, for what
made you stumble, then get stuck,
each time you began to read.
At the kitchen table, leaning over you,
she would say *focus, focus* as you
read aloud to her, tried again, again
to link written words together. At times
she grabbed hold of your shoulders
as if she could steer you
through the printed thickets
you always seemed to get lost in.

You too lacked words to tell us
how letters, like unfaithful pets,
sometimes turned on you,
how sentences loved to play tricks,
might suddenly jump off the page.

Today, long after you've
mastered your own special
way of reading, and long after I've
learned at last the word *dyslexia*,
you ask if I remember the night
we huddled between our beds

and listened in total darkness
to a transistor radio, trying our best
to get news of the approaching storm.

That, you say, is the way you often
strained to comprehend
the written world: reception
intermittent at best, then abruptly
noisy and distorted, only a few
clear words rising above the static.

HYMNS

For a moment we mistook it
for thunder, the sound
of those first furious chords
booming through the woods
behind our house. In unison,
we looked up from the porch
to re-check the Sunday
evening sky, surprised
to find it still shining clear.

This, followed by a cloudburst
of voices raining down
a rolling refrain of hallelujah
and hear my cry, Precious Lord,
so different from the tepid
drizzle of Methodist music
I'd huddled under that morning,
holding one half of the hymnal
I shared with my brother.

And even though it was almost
suppertime, I couldn't stop myself
from following that sound down
the long narrow path through tall
oaks and sweetgums to the clearing
in the center of which
was the unpainted church. Always
empty when I'd passed there
before, it was filled with people.

The tall paned windows were
thrown wide open and the shiny
black moons of faces lifted

above each sash. Hidden behind
a tree trunk, I waited through
a splatter of verses
for the repeated downpour
chorus to try on my singing voice
with words I knew by heart

though I'd never before heard them
sung like this. Belting out
the notes, I could feel the surge
of our hymn unclogging the gullies
and streams, flushing out dirt
and litter, beginning to wash
the whole world clean. I held
myself tight. All around me,
salvation rose like steam.

THE UPRIGHT

The older it got, the more it refused
to stay in tune for long. One note,
not-quite-right, a second that—insistently,
defiantly—plinked a little flat. Another
that might, in the middle of a scale,
suddenly squeak an octave or two
higher than it should.

He tried to keep the changes to himself,
blushed at every surprising warble
in his usually faultless playing,
choked back the giggle in one chord
of "Lead on, O King Eternal."

But one day, when he thought no one
was listening, he began to draw them
out—all the wild, crooked sounds—
fitting his fingers around each one,
hammering them repeatedly. Then he
waited, dreading repercussions, and
when none came, smiled and started again.

Alone in the hot pour
of an August afternoon, he grew even bolder,
began to fashion his own cacophonies,
accessorized Bach with noise
that surely would make the master frown.
Hidden here, within reach, were half-wrong
arpeggios he hurled like expletives
off mirror and mantel in the parlor.
He leaned his teenage body in,
hands learning to unzip
black keys, to dig into ivory

underthings. And then he stopped:
his mother at the door, the lock
sharply unlocked, the stiff
wooden stool beneath him
twisting a painful quarter-turn.

In the hallway she looked up,
called out, "Play me
something pretty." And before him,
wide grin of the keyboard, his
fingers poised on its lip.

MRS. LUNA

As soon as you understand
that in all my thirteen years
I'd never seen her, not once,
with her head uncovered, that
she had never—since the day
she was widowed—stepped outside
her front door without a black
wide-brimmed hat on,
could even be (for all we neighbors
knew) bald as an Easter egg on top,
then you'll know exactly
the way I watched Mrs. Luna
that August afternoon, half-hidden
by mimosa branches, as she
rocked slowly, slowly, hatless
on her back porch, sipping something
from a frosted glass,
and why I held my breath
when she lounged further down
in the chair, removed the tortoise-shell
comb and, chin lifted,
tossed back her head just enough
for a coil of silver-blonde
to come cascading down.

Oh, I'd never seen such hair!
It almost reached the floor,
captured all the light
sifting through the heavens. But
what I remember best is the sound
I heard when she reached in
with one hand, fingers starting
to dig through hair-roots—

short quick rubs
searching for an itch.

Perhaps it was nothing more
than noise from the street, wind
strumming the trees. That groan
or sigh released
the very moment I finally
exhaled: long slow *ahhh*
spiraling down
and repeating precisely
the shape her hair transcribed.

WAVES OF THE DANUBE

Mrs. Wallace counted out the steps
as we drove or dragged
our partners across the concrete
floor of the empty Farmers' Market,

becoming more frustrated with every
bungled turn, more befuddled each
time our feet got tangled in the boxes
of one-two-three, one-two-three,

until the needle on the record began
to scrape, scrape and Mrs. Wallace,
catching her breath, proclaimed one pair
the best dancers she'd ever taught.

Whispers and catcalls began
the minute we saw exactly who
she meant: Phillip the gangly kid
too tall for his pants, Marie the plump

one with pimples and braces.
Mrs. Wallace silenced us with her stare
and asked if the two of them would
please, as a gift to us all, show us

how a waltz should be waltzed.
For a few seconds, as the violins
began again to stir, they stood there
staring at one another. And though

his hand moved quickly to lock
behind her back, and her chin lifted
as if jerked up by a cord, their first steps
were tentative, a testing of the water.

We were ready to look away until
we witnessed, on a downbeat,
the moment they finally caught the wave
that swept them up above the floor.

In the days to come, we would find it
hard to speak to one another of the elegance
we'd seen, how they floated from crest
to crest then glided even higher, circling

the air above us. When at last they twirled
to a stop, even Mrs. Wallace was silent.
They'd gone somewhere we couldn't go.
Phillip took one wobbly step, as if

readjusting to the earth's pull. Marie blinked,
searching for bearings in this place where,
the very next morning, ham hocks
and turnip greens would be on display.

WHAT A PENNY BOUGHT

The vise of Mr. Sexton's arm
tightened around my waist,
hoisted me up
above the glass counter, high
enough to stare into the round
mouth of the giant Mason jar,
past peppers and cloves bobbing
on the surface, to the dark
muck beneath
which even shafts of sunlight
coming through the store's street-
front window failed to penetrate,
the place I'd seen long knobby
creatures hiding, submerged
side by side, across each other.

I held my breath against
the gusts of sharp vinegary air
and dipped in one shy finger,
slowly, until Mr. Sexton
hiked me up another
inch or two, his rough voice
grunting *hurry boy,*
and pick one. And then I did,
plunged my whole arm
deep into cool slime, my hand
opening, fitting at last
around the prize I pulled out: firm
fleshy pickle, its ooze
dripping on my shirt, on Mr. Sexton,
across the counter, the linoleum
floor. Outside, between bites,
I licked my fingers one by one

as sky and clouds, the distant
hills, all flared up
reckless and green.

THE POWERS OF KUDZU

He'd heard all the warnings: how
its vines could grow a foot or more
in a single summer day, could haul down
telephone lines, smother scrub-pine,
swallow a sweetgum whole.
Cocker spaniels had been lost in it,
they said, and a baby girl almost snared
in the loop of one thin tendril.

But when he looked at kudzu
long enough—alone, staring down
into the thick leafy weave between
Water Street and the railroad track—
it began to show him all
the objects hoarded in its deep green
pockets: bright chunks of coal, flakes
of mica, a set of rusted mattress
springs, flattened tin cans,
a hubcap jeweled in sunlight.

And whose eye was that
blinking through leaf shadow? Whose
gold tooth? He leaned further
and further over the embankment's
edge, balancing with his bike,
until its leaves reached out
to lick an ankle, until he caught himself
shivering all over.

SKIN-THE-CAT

I recognize that boy laughing
in the harness of his father's arms,
head upside-down, body doubled
over, small hands lost

in the larger ones. He thinks
he can hang there forever, bumping up
against the drum of ribs, in the fold
of that embrace, summer light

stretched to the point of breaking.
I can't remember if it's
the pinch of twisted shoulders
or blood rushing to his face

that finally demands
he unwind himself, tips him
toward that first unbuckling:
feet launched ceilingward, then over,

one body somersaulting out
of the other, until the boy's returned
to ground, to the life
he's just begun to recognize as his.

BLUE

There were days by the lake,
alone in a porch swing,
when I was so in love
with the ambiguous
I refused to look up, even once,
at the absolute blue of sky,
stared straight ahead
at distant hills neither green
nor gray, at water neither gray
nor blue, and told myself
the reeds beside the shore,
swaying slightly, were a color
that defied naming even
as the shallow pool behind them
went on reflecting
its one clear shade of yellow.

BELOW THE SURFACE

On his back, staring up
at sunlight reflected off the lake
onto the leafy underbelly of a white oak,
he thinks this is precisely what
carp and catfish must see when
they eye the water's surface
from below: the heavens shimmering
above them, wavy lines of light
framing patches of dark
that could be mosquito or leaf
but paler than that, leaving
no trace as they shift, dissolve,

are briefly blotted out
by the shadow of clouds or wings,
or turn into flames, gold rivulets
almost blinding, a flickering conflagration
extinguished only by some
new stillness, the sky pressing down,
the surface suddenly transparent
allowing the centers of light
to hold like stars, to arrange
themselves into constellations bright
enough to dazzle the creatures below
into feverish dreams of flight.

LOST BIRD

The morning his prize parakeet
threaded a brief opening of the birdhouse
door and vanished over trees,
my father couldn't stop staring
at the vacant lot of sky. That's how
I found him: blue electric eyes
trained due south, as if each pivot,
each swoop the bird had made
was firmly committed to memory
and any minute now he'd think of a way
to run the scene in reverse. Re-focus
the glittery green dot mid-center
the horizon, reconstruct the shallow "v"
he'd seen pumping over distant pines.
Then he'd reel it back in
past sweetgum, pecan branches,
yaupon hedge. Even further: until
he felt the frantic quiver of wings
pressed against his palm.

Once I watched him dissect flight
from a parakeet's wing. Pinning
the bird's back to the floor, he forced open
gathered plumage, cut in half
the long end-feathers one by one.
Then carefully, with steel clippers, he snipped
the rows of down growing along the gristle.
How I wanted that bird to fight him
or shriek, shriek
instead of just lying there, its eye
half closed, the same stupid look on its face
as on the parakeets I saw him haul
inside in foot-square cages,

all the while wooing them with words
whispered under his breath. He knew
how to reduce his voice to tones,
to low, limpid vowels
more animal than thought,
more charm than story,
could fold his music into plump,
two-footed vows intoned
through the bars of a cage:
hel-lo, sweetie,
pret-ty boy, crooning them over and over

until the bird tilted its head slightly,
clutched, unclutched the wooden perch.
The feathers of its throat
pulsed once, again,
and then, with no expression,
it began to speak,
mimicking the very voice my father
used to address the still-empty sky
that morning the bird got away:
fool-ish, fool-ish waste.

When we turned at last toward the house,
his hand gripped my shoulder.
I could taste in the back of my mouth
the words he'd have me say:
too free
too free,
though the sounds I tried to make
were drowned out at that moment
by noise rising from the birdhouse
where, for no apparent reason,
dozens of parakeets burst into wing,
eddies of blue and yellow
skittering upwards, squawking,

thrashing from feeder to boxes, smacking
against the wire-mesh
walls—fifteen feet tall
and dizzy by then with light.

ADOLESCENCE

Anyone could take that Western Flyer,
upended all week behind my neighbor's garage,
for an emblem of defeat: its handlebars
pinned to the ground, chain snapped in two,
sprocket rusting, a thin white towel
spread out beneath it like a banner in surrender.
A sad zinc taste floods my mouth each time
its wheels, pointed skyward, begin
to spin slowly in opposite directions.

I remember, as a pale and scrawny
fourteen year old, feeling stranded in a universe
of bigger men who were hairier, mysterious,
who coasted naked across the steamy field
of the locker room, filled the air with flying
jockstraps and jokes I didn't understand. I tried
to hide my pre-pubescent ugliness
under giant towels, pedaled cautiously through
shadows, terrified of the powerful, forbidden
urges threatening to spin out of control. I prayed
no one would notice I didn't belong there,
tried to keep my balance, to ride out the changes.

RAMON

You must know a Ramon. He's not
the one unless you once were told
never to go near him, unless
you've spent entire days imagining
his murky past, have waited up
to catch a glimpse of him
stepping out of a shiny red Impala
into the streetlight's gleam,
white shirt worn open, dark trousers
with no belt, unless you still
can hear his whiskey voice
calling to a wife no one ever saw.

And so tonight, crossing the lobby
of Hotel Alhambra, you turn at once
to face the woman in a flouncy
dress who calls out his name
and, barely hesitating, calls again,
rolling the "r" longer, louder.
It's then you realize
there's no one else around: she
must be speaking to you (*yes, you!*),
but almost too quickly, you shake
your head and walk away, only
to discover, as the elevator doors
snap shut, that your gaze

is suddenly transfixed by the image
on the mirrored wall in front of you,
vibrating now at high speed
as you ascend, electrons altering
their paths, whole molecules shifting
until what is reflected

begins to conform to the name
still echoing in your head, to the memory
it recalls which, simultaneously,
has undergone a subtle transformation

so that when you step into the soft
glow of the fourteenth floor,
every part of you has changed: Ramon,
creature who struts across the wild
flowered pattern of the carpet,
fingers sleeking back his hair, delicious
accent in the greeting
offered a couple passing by who
glance back, almost stare
at the one whose shadow stretches
endlessly down the hallway,
the one with skin darker, more luminous
than seemed possible just
minutes ago, the one
with the piano keyboard grin
and two green cockatiels for eyes.

SMALL TOWN MYTH

In early morning light, observed
through the wide picture window
of Willoughby's Funeral Home,
she looked not so fearsome,
not so strong, even a bit comical:
pale department store mannequin
propped up against the far parlor wall,
wrapped in a shiny white choir robe,
the winglike attachments to her
shoulders covered with goose down
and glittery fringe, circle of tinseled
wire sprouting from her silver-blond wig,

though by noon, in the junior high
cafeteria, when I told my friends
what I'd seen on my way to school,
I heard myself give her a name—
The Death Angel—proclaim how I'd
seen her floating in air, both arms
outstretched above an open coffin,
how music could be heard, just barely,
arising from an organ I couldn't
exactly see, how the perfect "O"
of her mouth seemed ready to speak
of another world, an outer dark,

but even I was not prepared
for the moment that very night when,
piled into an older friend's blue Chevy,
the six of us watched the beam
of our headlights angle through
Willoughby's window in such a way
we suddenly beheld her reaching out

to us, the blaze of her halo
and wings lighting up a man's body
laid out below until the car exploded
into high-pitched screams rising
above howls of laughter, and

yet by the next morning our shouts
had become less shrill, our words
more earnest with each recounting
until the boy who was riding shotgun
began to swear She had fixed Her eyes
on him alone, and the girl in the back seat,
the one who screamed longest and loudest,
proclaimed she'd seen Her again, this time
sweeping low across the river, and I couldn't
help but retell my ailing grandfather's
account of how The Death Angel hovered
above his bed, spoke to him in dreams.

NIGHT WATCH

In a far corner of the ICU waiting room
the ancient rusted-grey radiator
has been wailing all night: a pounding
squall, followed by high-pitched shrieks.

The three of us, near strangers,
lined up along the wall
in scooped-out fiberglass chairs, pitch
our voices just loud enough
to be heard above it. Sipping coffee,
we speak of heart attacks and cancer,
calling messages to one another
as if across a frozen lake. Then each of us,
in courteous sequence, glances up
at the clock that rules the opposite wall.
One by one we cross the room,
walk toward our own reflection in the dark
curtainless window—first the elderly
man in the green plaid coat,
next the mother clutching her fistful
of tissue, then me.

Below the window, a line of thin figures
slips elusively between trees, turns
into headlights sweeping
the parking lot fence. The long,
long shadow of the night watchman
grows shorter, shorter as he approaches
a streetlamp, his breath
ghosting the air. Down the hall,
you swallow oxygen through a tube.
In an hour or so, day will start throbbing up,

mirrored on our faces, glinting off
windshields.

I turn in time to see the young man
in a blue coat, oil-stained,
nod as he marches across the room.
He kneels in the corner before the ailing
radiator and then, with a wrench, reaches in.

WHILE WE WAIT FOR THE DEMEROL TO WORK

The slow prayer of a sculling boat
is drifting forward on its own,
against the Potomac's urging,
oars uplifted. From your window
I watch it tug open
the tight zipper of river,
can almost count the knots
along the arms of rowers
who hold back just
a moment longer. How they must
ache to start again
the linked dip and pull, soft stroke
across the water's smooth brow.

THE PROJECTIONIST'S SON

In the balcony dark, in my usual
seat outside his booth, I'd
sometimes get bored by a love scene
flickering on the screen below
or frightened by the eight-armed
monster rising from the Deep,
and would tap on his door to ask
if I could sit with him awhile. But
once I slipped in quietly
and found him asleep in his chair,
sprockets ticking as the story
unspooled, a soft blue light
spilling all around him.

Now that he's dead, he sometimes
follows me into moviehouses.
I can hear him in the seat next
to me, mumbling above the music,
unable to sit still. Or he
shows up late, out of breath,
halfway through the feature
presentation. Stepping over me,
he stubs my toe, spills popcorn
on my lap. And even before
I can ask how he's been
all these years, he turns to me
with that anxious puzzled look,
begging to be told
everything he's missed.

INFIDELITIES

Whisper it to yourself:
you have betrayed him.

This morning you found yourself
suddenly in love
with the tattered music of a jay
bullying the air outside your window.
Enraptured, you failed to be reminded
of what he might have said.

Later, you listened to footsteps
crossing the front porch
and did not (not even for a second)
mistake them for his. You picked up
the catalog dropped through the slot
and casually read his name
printed on the label, refusing
this time to be led back
to the prison yard of memory.

This much is certain:
your infidelities will change you.

Like a sweater you've worn too long
the sadness will grow loose. Gone
the old chafing at your neckline,
familiar musk of sweat and wool.
And you will miss it.

You'll suddenly stop needing
to worry the world into meaning.
One afternoon the clock will

simply say three fifteen, the light
on the windowsill will say only winter.

You'll begin to imagine a morning
when the calm that sometimes
stretches across the front lawn
will include even you.

One night you will listen
to the toolshed door open and close,
open, close, like the arguments
you had before his death slammed shut
the door for good. But, falling asleep,
you'll think *only the wind.*

WHITE HIBISCUS

He is waving down to me, pale cheek
pressed against the windowpane
until his face is out of focus,
white penny, moonstone set
high in a window, within a tower
of windows. Wilson Sanitorium,
all the windows shut tight,
his window, five up, third over:
one hand moves slowly, arms almost lost
in the floating dark square.

My older brother and I
are not allowed up the stairs. Mother
explains to us: "He's up there
fighting T.B." But what has T.B. done
to make our father so angry? Around us,
rows of shrubs are lit up
with flowers and, on the lawn,
white petals lie crushed underfoot.
I pick them by the armful, loving
the way the giant bumblebees love them,
loving the ruby tongues
in the center of all that white.

And now I hold both hands,
stuffed with blossoms, high above my head.
I think I see him smile: white fist,
white bud, small and far away
at first, it begins to unfold
from the the thin, dark stems of his arms.

BRIGHT LEAF

Entering, my grandfather bowed
his head, the barn's opening
so low I could hook my fingers
on top of the doorjamb and lean
just my face into a sweet blast
of nightshade, the air even hotter
and drier than the dog day afternoon.

The beam of his flashlight
bounced off the flue's
blue-white jets, then jerked
upwards in short, bright arcs
as he moved toward the inner
ladder, began the slow, careful climb.

High above him, thermometers
suspended strategically from rafter
and beam told how far
to raise or lower the flame, how long
it took to turn green into gold.

I watched until his boots rose
into the vaulted ceiling, lifted
past rack after crisscrossed rack
of leaves that quivered in his wake
like giant saffron moths
nesting side by side
on thin wooden poles, wings
folded behind them in their sleep.